j
P
A

912-1786

Andersen, Hans Christian
The emperor's new clothes

DATE DUE   21st Ed,

DATE DUE	DATE DUE		
JY 09 '97	MR 14 01		
AG 6 '97	OC 02 02		
JY -1 '98	JA 15 '03		
OC 21 '98	AG 06 03		
FE 24 '99	JY 14 '04		
JE 02 '99	MAR 0 5 2008		
JY 21 '99	APR 0 7 2010		
AP 05 00			
MY 03 '00			
AG 16 00			

DEMCO

HANS CHRISTIAN ANDERSEN

The Emperor's New Clothes

RETOLD BY RIKI LEVINSON

ILLUSTRATED BY

ROBERT BYRD

DUTTON CHILDREN'S BOOKS   NEW YORK

Library of Congress Cataloging-in-Publication Data
Levinson, Riki.
The emperor's new clothes / Hans Christian Andersen;
retold by Riki Levinson.—1st ed.
p. cm.
Summary: Two rascals sell a vain emperor an invisible suit
of clothes.
ISBN 0-525-44611-7
[1. Fairy tales.] I. Andersen, H. C. (Hans Christian),
1805–1875. Kejserens nye klæder. II. Title.
PZ8.L4794Em   1990
[E]—dc20   89-23820 CIP AC

Published in the United States by Dutton Children's Books,
a division of Penguin Books USA Inc.
Printed in Hong Kong by South China Printing Co.
First Edition   10 9 8 7 6 5 4 3 2 1

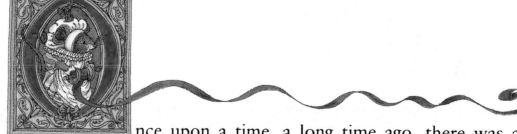

nce upon a time, a long time ago, there was an Emperor who lived in a beautiful palace.

He did not care about his soldiers or his many subjects. He cared only about himself.

The Emperor especially loved his clothes. He paraded through

the palace and in the royal courtyard in every new outfit so that
all could admire him. He was very vain.

One day two strangers came to the town and went directly to the palace gate.

"We wish to see the Emperor," one of them said to the guards. "Would you kindly take our letter to the Emperor's Minister?"

A guard took their letter to the Royal Minister.

When the Minister read the strangers' letter, he hurried to the Lord High Chamberlain.

When the Chamberlain read it, he hurried to the Emperor, for he knew that His Royal Highness would want to meet these men.

The strangers professed to be the most able weavers in the land. They claimed to weave cloth with gold and silver thread of extraordinary beauty and fineness. In fact, their cloth was so fine that it would be invisible to anyone who was stupid or unfit for office.

I must see these weavers, the Emperor thought. I would have clothes even more beautiful than I have now! And I could find out who is dull-witted or truly unfit for office. What a remarkable test this would prove to be.

"BRING THEM HERE!" roared the Emperor.

"Minister, send for the weavers!" ordered the Chamberlain.
"Guards, send for the weavers!" ordered the Minister.

When the strangers came before the Emperor, they described the extraordinary cloth that only they could weave.

The Emperor listened intently. He believed them.

"MAGNIFICENT!" bellowed the Emperor. "Give these fine men whatever they need."

"Minister!" ordered the Chamberlain. "Take them to a palace room."

"Guards!" ordered the Minister. "Escort these men to their quarters."

The next day the weavers bought a big loom and shuttles.
They bought small coffers to hold the gold and silver thread,
and two large trunks to store the woven cloth. But they did not
buy more than a few spools of thread, for the weavers were
truly scoundrels.

Every day they sat at their loom pretending to weave.

And at night, after everyone was asleep, they took out the
money they had not spent and counted it again and again.

As the days passed, the Emperor wondered what the cloth
looked like.
So he sent his loyal Minister to see the weavers.

The Minister watched them working at the empty loom. He stood there, unable to speak. I do not see any cloth. Can *I* not see it because I am stupid? he wondered with horror.

The scoundrels saw the shocked expression on the Minister's face.

Quickly, one of them asked, "Aren't these the most beautiful colors and patterns you've ever seen?"

The Minister nodded. "Uh . . . of charming color . . . quite beautiful . . ." he sputtered, not knowing what else to say.

"We will need more money—to buy more thread," the other scoundrel said.

As the Minister hurried back to the Emperor, he wondered what he should say. He knew that he could not tell the truth—that *he* could not see the cloth.

"Your Royal Highness," said the Minister as he bowed to the Emperor.

"How does the cloth look?" asked the Emperor anxiously. "Is it extraordinarily beautiful?"

"Your Highness," answered the Minister, "you would not believe what I have just seen."

The Emperor was pleased.

A week passed. The impatient Emperor summoned his Chamberlain.

"My loyal Chamberlain, you know that I trust you," the Emperor said. "Go to the weavers and report on their progress. I am anxious to have a new outfit made for the festival."

The Chamberlain hurried to the weaving room.

He saw one scoundrel working feverishly at the empty loom. The other scoundrel was folding the imaginary cloth. "Sire," he said, "feel this cloth. Isn't it the finest, the lightest ever made?"

The Chamberlain was dumbfounded, but he put his hand out as if to touch the cloth. "It is so light, one cannot even feel it," he said, not knowing what else to say.

The scoundrels grinned happily.

"Sire," said the scoundrel at the loom, "we are almost finished weaving. Next week we will make the Emperor's new outfit. It will be ready for the festival."

Slowly, the Chamberlain went back to the royal room. He could not confess to the Emperor that *he* did not see or feel the cloth, for the Emperor would think him stupid and unfit for his high office.

The Emperor rushed to greet him. "And how did you find their work?" he asked anxiously.

"Your Highness," answered the Chamberlain, "there are no words to describe what I have just seen."

The Emperor was very pleased.

Word spread throughout the town that the weavers would
soon have enough cloth for their Emperor's new outfit.

Crowds of villagers gathered below the windows of the weaving room. They watched the weavers moving about quickly, but they could not see the cloth.

On the morning of the festival day, the Chamberlain and the Minister waited with the Emperor in the royal dressing room.

The weavers entered the room with their arms stretched out in front of them as if they were holding the imaginary clothes.

The Emperor stared at them. His face reddened. His eyes bulged. But he did not say a word.

The weavers placed the imaginary new clothes carefully on the table. Then they turned and bowed to the Emperor.

The stunned Emperor still could not speak. My loyal Chamberlain and wise Minister have seen this extraordinary cloth. How can I say that *I* cannot? the foolish Emperor thought.

"Your Highness," one scoundrel said, "would you kindly un-
dress so that we may fit your new outfit?"

The Emperor, very upset, rushed behind the screen and took
off his clothes.

"First the pantaloons," the other scoundrel said. He took a piece from the imaginary pile of clothes and passed it to the Emperor. Then he waited a moment and asked, "Tell me, Your Royal Highness, don't these pantaloons feel as light as a feather?"

"Extraordinary," the Emperor lied.

"And now the shirt," said the other scoundrel, passing another imaginary piece to the Emperor. "Doesn't this too fit well?"

"Ah yes," the Emperor answered. Then he came out from behind the screen.

The Emperor looked at the Chamberlain and the Minister. They nodded to him as if approvingly.

The scoundrels hugged each other, gleefully.

"And here is your beautiful coat edged with gold and silver thread. Come to the mirror and let us help you put it on," said one of the scoundrels.

They helped the Emperor put on his imaginary coat.

"Isn't it as fine as we promised?" asked one of the scoundrels.

"Ah yes," the Emperor answered. He turned this way and that way in front of the mirror as if admiring the coat. "It is extraordinarily beautiful."

"And now for our greatest achievement—your robe," said the other scoundrel. "See the diamond pattern from collar to hem?"

"Magnificent! Is it not?" he asked his Chamberlain and Minister.

The Chamberlain nodded, not knowing what to say. "Minister, we are ready."

"We are ready," said the Minister.

"LET THE PROCESSION BEGIN!" bellowed the Emperor.

They left the royal quarters and went down the palace steps into the courtyard.

Trumpets blared.

Royal guards held a velvet canopy over the Emperor as he led the procession.

The Chamberlain followed, holding the train of the Emperor's imaginary robe.

The Minister followed the Chamberlain.

And then came the scoundrels, for the Emperor wanted all to see the master weavers who had made his new outfit.

Crowds of villagers pressed forward to see their Emperor.

My villagers are not their usual noisy selves, the Emperor thought, wondering why they were so quiet. Ah, it must be because they have never seen me wearing such extraordinarily beautiful clothes before.

The Emperor stopped before his loyal subjects.

Suddenly, a little one pushed forward between an elder villager's legs.

"The Emperor is naked," the little one said.

"Be quiet, child," warned a villager.

"Quiet!" hissed a guard.

"But he is not wearing anything," the little one said truthfully.

The villagers nodded and whispered to one another. "Our Emperor is naked," they said.

"ONWARD!" roared the Emperor. "Let all the villagers see our royal person."

"Minister, let us continue!" the Chamberlain ordered.

"Forward, guards!" ordered the Minister.

The royal procession moved on through the town.

The vain and foolish Emperor, with head held high proudly, waved to everyone as he passed by.